小熊，
我們一齊幹吧

馬丁·沃德爾 文

巴巴拉·弗思 圖

This edition published in 1996 by
Magi Publications
22 Manchester Street, London W1M 5PG

Text © Martin Waddell, 1996
Illustrations © Barbara Firth, 1996
Copyright © Chinese translation, Magi Publications, 1996

First published in Great Britain in 1996 by
Walker Books Ltd, London

Printed and bound in Italy

ISBN 1 85430 519 0

YOU AND ME, LITTLE BEAR

by Martin Waddell

illustrated by Barbara Firth

Translated by East Word

從前有兩隻熊，個子大的叫 "大熊"，

個子小的叫 "小熊"。

小熊喜歡玩耍，而大熊卻總是

有事需要去幹。

Once there were two bears,
Big Bear and Little Bear.
Big Bear is the big bear and Little Bear
is the little bear.
Little Bear wanted to play, but Big Bear
      had things to do.

小熊説： "我想玩!"

"我現在得去弄些劈柴來取暖，" 大熊説。

"我也去弄點兒來，" 小熊説。

"小熊，我們一齊幹吧。我們一起去

樹林裡找吧，" 大熊説。

"I want to play!" Little Bear said.
"I've got to get wood for the fire,"
said Big Bear.
"I'll get some too," Little Bear said.
"You and me, Little Bear," said Big Bear.
"We'll fetch the wood in together!"

小熊問：　"我們現在該幹甚麼呢？"

"我要去打水，" 大熊説。

小熊問：　"我可以去嗎？"

"小熊，我們一齊幹吧，" 大熊説。 "我們一起

去打水吧!"

"What shall we do now?" Little Bear asked.
"I'm going for water," said Big Bear.
"Can I come too?" Little Bear asked.
"You and me, Little Bear," said Big Bear.
"We'll go for the water together."

"現在我們可以玩了吧，" 小熊説。

"我還需要收拾屋子呢，" 大熊説。

"好吧……我也來收拾，" 小熊説。

"小熊，我們一齊幹吧。你把你的東西收拾好，

小熊。剩下的我來收拾，" 大熊説。

"Now we can play," Little Bear said.
"I've still got to tidy our cave," said Big Bear.
"Well . . . I'll tidy too!" Little Bear said.
"You and me," said Big Bear. "You tidy your
things, Little Bear. I'll look after the rest."

小熊説：“我已經把我的東西收拾好了，大熊！”

“很好，小熊，”大熊説。“可我還沒收拾完呢。”

小熊説：“我想讓你也來玩！”

“你還是自己玩吧，小熊，”大熊説。“我還有

很多事要做呢。”於是，小熊獨自去玩了，大熊繼續幹活。

"I've tidied my things, Big Bear!" Little Bear said.
"That's good, Little Bear," said Big Bear. "But I'm
not finished yet."
"I want you to play!" Little Bear said.
"You'll have to play by yourself,
Little Bear," said Big Bear.
"I've still got plenty to do!"
Little Bear went to play by
himself, while Big Bear
got on with the work.

小熊玩
"熊跳板"。

Little Bear played
bear-jump.

小熊玩
"熊滑梯"。

Little Bear played
bear-slide.

小熊玩
"熊揪扦" 。

**Little Bear played
bear-swing.**

小熊玩

"小樹枝把戲" 。

**Little Bear played
bear-tricks-with-bear-sticks.**

小熊玩"熊倒立";

大熊出來坐在外面的石頭上。

小熊玩"熊打轉";大熊閉上眼睛想心事。

Little Bear played bear-stand-on-his-head and
Big Bear came out to sit on his rock.
Little Bear played
bear-run-about-by-
himself and Big
Bear closed his
eyes for a think.

小熊去和大熊說話，但是，

大熊卻……

睡著了！

Little Bear went to speak
to Big Bear, but
Big Bear was . . .

asleep!

小熊喊道: "醒醒、醒醒,大熊!"

大熊睜開雙眼。

"我已玩遍了我自己所有的遊戲," 小熊説。

"Wake up, Big Bear!" Little Bear said.
Big Bear opened his eyes.
"I've played all my games by myself,"
Little Bear said.

大熊想了想，説：　"小熊，讓我們玩捉迷藏。"

"我藏你找，" 小熊説。於是小熊跑開找地方

藏了起來。

Big Bear thought for a bit, then he said,
"Let's play hide-and-seek, Little Bear."
"I'll hide and you seek,"
　　Little Bear said, and he
　　ran off to hide.

大熊喊道：“我來啦!”

大熊找呀找呀，終於發現了小熊。

"I'm coming now!" Big Bear
called and he looked till he
found Little Bear.

輪到大熊藏小熊找了。

"我發現你啦!" 小熊喊道。 "現在又輪到我藏了。"

Then Big Bear hid, and Little Bear looked.
"I found you, Big Bear!" Little Bear said.
"Now I'll hide again."

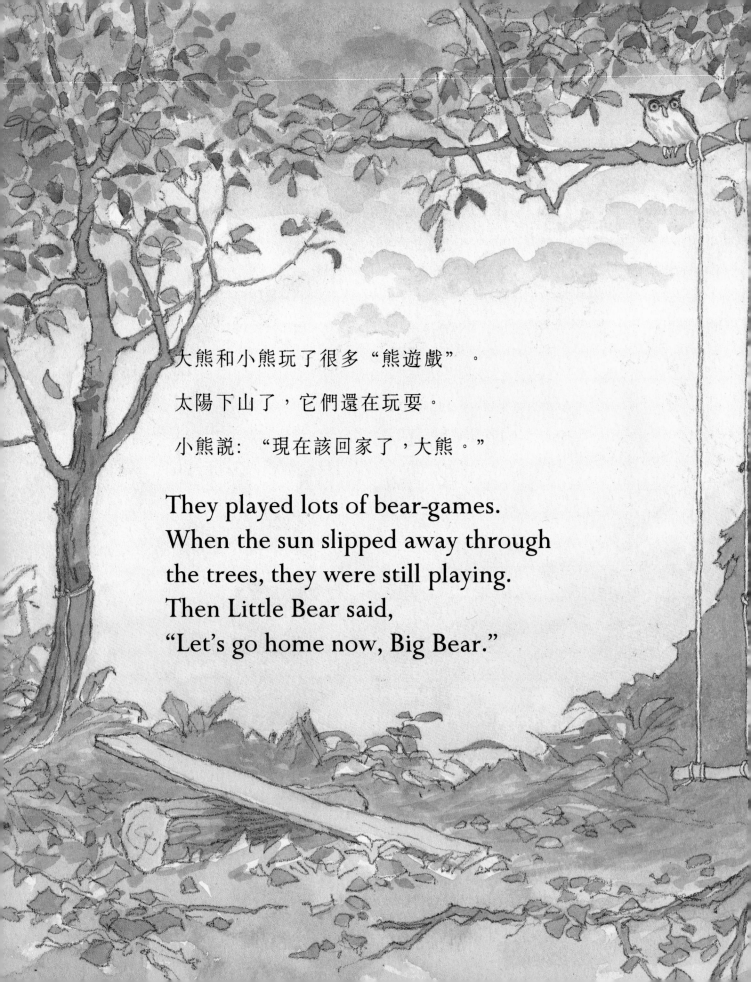

大熊和小熊玩了很多 "熊遊戲" 。

太陽下山了，它們還在玩耍。

小熊說： "現在該回家了，大熊。"

They played lots of bear-games.
When the sun slipped away through
the trees, they were still playing.
Then Little Bear said,
"Let's go home now, Big Bear."

大熊和小熊一起回家。

大熊說：“我們忙了一整天，小熊!”

“真開心了，大熊，”小熊說。“你和我……

Big Bear and Little Bear went
home to their cave.
"We've been busy today, Little Bear!"
said Big Bear.
"It was lovely, Big Bear," Little Bear said.
"Just you and me playing . . .

一起玩。"
together."